What a Scare,
Jesse Bear

What a Scare, Jesse Bear

BOO BY JESSE

by **Nancy White Carlstrom**

illustrated by **Bruce Degen**

Aladdin Paperbacks
New York London Toronto Sydney Singapore

OTHER BOOKS IN THE JESSE BEAR SERIES
BY NANCY WHITE CARLSTROM, ILLUSTRATED BY BRUCE DEGEN

Jesse Bear, What Will You Wear?
Better Not Get Wet, Jesse Bear
It's About Time, Jesse Bear
How Do You Say It Today, Jesse Bear?
Happy Birthday, Jesse Bear!
Let's Count It Out, Jesse Bear
Guess Who's Coming, Jesse Bear
Where is Christmas, Jesse Bear?

First Aladdin Paperbacks edition September 2002
Text copyright © 1999 by Nancy White Carlstrom
Illustrations copyright © 1999 by Bruce Degen

ALADDIN PAPERBACKS
An imprint of Simon & Schuster
Children's Publishing Division
1230 Avenue of the Americas
New York, NY 10020

Also available in a Simon & Schuster Books for Young Readers hardcover edition.
Designed by Anahid Hamparian.
The text of this book was set in 18-point Goudy.
The illustrations were rendered in pen-and-ink and watercolor.
Printed in Hong Kong
2 4 6 8 10 9 7 5 3 1

The Library of Congress has cataloged the hardcover edition as follows:
Carlstrom, Nancy White.
What a scare, Jesse Bear! / by Nancy White Carlstrom ; illustrated by Bruce Degen.
p. cm.
Summary: At Halloween Jesse Bear picks out a pumpkin,
helps make a jack-o-lantern, works on a costume, and has fun trick-or-treating.
ISBN 0-689-81961-7 (hc.)
[1. Bears—Fiction. 2. Halloween—Fiction. 3. Stories in rhyme.] I. Degen, Bruce, ill. II. Title.
PZ8.3.C21684We 1999
[E]—dc21
98-22087
CIP
AC
ISBN 0-689-85190-1 (Aladdin pbk.)

For Carolie and Jeff,
Allyson, Maddy, and Wyatt Brown
With love,
—N. W. C.

For Chris,
The Queen of Halloween
—B. D.

Halloween is coming,
Time for us to go
Out into the country,
Where the pumpkins grow.

Papa, Jesse, Grandma
Riding in the car
To a pick-your-pumpkin farm.
Hope it's not too far!

Let's pick out a pumpkin,
Which one will it be?
Big or little, in-between,
How about all three?

Papa draws a spooky face
And carves it carefully.

Then I get to scoop it out,
An ooey-gooey ME!

Let's turn out the light
And make a moaning sound.
Here comes Mama Bear—oh!
Surprises all around.

What a scare, Jesse Bear!

Let's work on the costume,
Lots of scraps and bits.
Dress-up clothes from long ago,
I hope that something fits.

Papa puts a black cape on
And some vampire teeth.
Mama wears a velvet coat
And tutu underneath.

I can try on many hats
And do a little dance
In curly wig and big red nose
And saggy baggy pants.

I think I'll wear a scary mask
With long and stringy hair,
Glowing eyes and wrinkled skin,
I'll be a monster bear.

I peek into the mirror
But I don't like what I see.
A truly frightening stranger
Is staring back at me.

What a scare, Jesse Bear!

Out into the darkness,
Shadows everywhere.

Let's all keep together,
Halloween is in the air!

Down the street we go
Making quite a sight,

Shivering and shaking
On trick-or-treating night.

Who are all these creatures?
No one looks the same.
They screech and scream and yell out, "Boo!"
How do they know my name?

What a scare, Jesse Bear!

Back at the next-door neighbors,
They've been waiting all night long
To make us laugh out loud
At their wobbly goblin song.

I want to put my mask on now
In this familiar place.
I'm ready to be brave enough
To wear this freaky face.

Home again, let's play a trick
And in the back way sneak,

Then we make the biggest fright
And hear the biggest EEEK!

What a scare, Jesse Bear!